A Rookie reader®

Bears, Bears, Everywhere

Written by Rita Milios

Illustrated by Keiko Motoyama

Children's Press®
A Division of Scholastic Inc.
New York • Toronto • London • Auckland • Sydney
Mexico City • New Delhi • Hong Kong
Danbury, Connecticut

For Yuri and Miho

—K.M.

Reading Consultants

Linda Cornwell
Literacy Specialist

Katharine A. Kane
Education Consultant
(Retired, San Diego County Office of Education
and San Diego State University)

Library of Congress Cataloging-in-Publication Data

Milios, Rita.
Bears, bears, everywhere / written by Rita Milios ; illustrated by Keiko Motoyama.
p. cm. — (Rookie reader)
Summary: A young girl finds bears everywhere and counts them, one to ten.
ISBN 0-516-22847-1 (lib. bdg.) 0-516-27830-4 (pbk.)
1. Counting—Juvenile literature. 2. Bears—Juvenile literature.
[1. Counting. 2. Bears.] I. Motoyama, Keiko, ill. II. Title. III. Series.
QA113 .M52 2003
513.2'11—dc21 2002008786

7 8 9 10 11 R 14 13 12 11 10 09 62

One bear in the air.

Two bears on the stairs.

Look! I see three in a tree.

There are four more
behind the door.

Five bears in a chair.

Bears, bears, everywhere.

Six bears wearing pajamas.

Seven bears crying
for their mamas.

Eight bears hungry as can be.

Nine bears running after me.

Bears here.

Bears there.

Bears, bears, everywhere.

Ten bears huffing and puffing.

I'm so glad they're
full of stuffing.

Word List (53 words)

a	eight	mamas	stairs
after	everywhere	me	stuffing
air	five	more	ten
and	for	nine	the
are	four	of	their
as	full	on	there
be	glad	one	they're
bear	here	pajamas	three
bears	huffing	puffing	tree
behind	hungry	running	two
can	I	see	wearing
chair	I'm	seven	
crying	in	six	
door	look	so	

About the Author

Rita Milios is a freelance writer and editor of more than two dozen books and numerous magazine articles. She writes both fiction and nonfiction for children in kindergarten to eighth grade. She has her Masters in Social Work and is also an educational consultant and psychotherapist. Milios often speaks at conferences to students, teachers, and writers. She has two grown children and lives with her husband in Toledo, Ohio.

About the Illustrator

Keiko Motoyama graduated from the Art Center College of Design in California. She has worked as a greeting card designer and has illustrated many books for children. She lives in Rancho Palos Verdes, California, with her husband and two daughters.